THE SUBSTITUTE KID

By Joseph K. Smith

PUBLISH AMERICA

PublishAmerica

Baltimore

First printing

All characters in this book are fictitious, and any resemblance to real persons,
living or dead, is coincidental.

PublishAmerica has allowed this work to remain exactly as the author intended,
verbatim, without editorial input.

ISBN: 1-60672-272-7
PUBLISHED BY PUBLISHAMERICA, LLLP
www.publishamerica.com
Baltimore

Printed in the United States of America

For my niece, Michaela Ardagna, the *real* Michaela:
The inspiration for this story.

Thank you to my wife, Catherine, without your help and constant nagging this story would never have seen the light of day.

Thanks also to Nancy Butts for your endless guidance and editing of this story.

A big hearty thanks goes out to the town of North Andover. Your great inspiration for this book will forever remain in my heart.

Chapter 1

"OK, Jessica, this is the moment you've been waiting for. I'm going to tell you what I have planned for this afternoon."

A big smile came across Jessica's face. "You really know how to torture me, don't you?"

Jessica was my best friend. She was short, and had long blonde hair and crystal blue eyes.

"I think you'll agree it was worth the wait," I said.

"I'll decide if it was worth it."

"Two days ago when I was walking home from school, I cut through the woods and found something that you might like."

"What was it?"

"Are you sure you want to know?"

"Tell me right now, Michaela."

"I found a nest of baby robins in an oak tree."

"No way, really?"

I knew Jessica loved birds. Her grandmother used to take her bird watching when she was little, and she had always talked about how much fun they had together. Jessica's love for birds had grown stronger after her granny's death, a year earlier.

"Yes, there was a mother bird and six babies in the nest. The babies were so tiny."

"Well, let's go and find it," Jessica said.

We made our way to the woods, which were right behind the school, as the afternoon sky grew a deep gray. It looked like we might be getting some rain anytime. As we entered the woods, I heard some weird noises.

Eek, Eek, Eek!

"What was that?" Jessica asked.

Before I had time to answer her question, we heard.

Ark, Ark, Ark!

Jessica turned to me and grabbed my arm. "What was that noise?"

"Oh, it's probably just some birds, or an owl."

"I've never heard any birds that sound like that."

Now she was getting me worried. I could barely see five feet in front of us and I had kind of forgotten where the nest was.

"I think we need to go to the left."

"What do you mean, you think?" Jessica asked.

"I kind of forgot exactly where the birds are."

"Michaela, I'm getting scared. You had better find this nest, and fast!"

Jessica had barely finished her sentence as we saw three figures, up ahead, run past us.

"What was that?" Jessica asked.

"I have no clue."

"I'm scared. I want to get out of here."

"We can't leave yet. I know we are getting close to the nest."

Jessica pressed the illumination button on her watch and said, "If you don't find the nest within the next five minutes, we are out of here. And I'm timing you."

"Fine. I will definitely find it before then, stop worrying."

Suddenly, three monsters jumped out from behind the trees and started chasing us.

"Run for your life!" shouted Jessica.

We ran as fast as we could. The monsters had large silver heads, with big fangs coming out of their mouths. I couldn't make out much more than that in the darkness, and I didn't want to stop running to take a better look.

"Hurry up, Jessica. I can see the edge of the woods."

The sun was coming out and I could see the rays beaming through the tree limbs.

"Just make it out of the woods!" I yelled. "I don't think they will follow us out into the street."

I looked behind. Jessica was still trailing me, and the monsters were not far behind.

"They are going to catch me," Jessica said.

One of the monsters leaped for Jessica's ankle, but as he did, he tripped and this made the other two monsters crash, and they all rolled to the ground. I made it to the edge of the woods, and ran out into the street; Jessica was not far behind me.

We both turned back and I noticed something strange. The monsters were all wearing sneakers.

"Hey, Jessica, something is weird about those monsters. They are all wearing Nikes."

Jessica turned back, while she huffed and puffed. "You are right, they are wearing Nikes."

The tallest monster took off what appeared to be a mask, and the other two followed.

"It's my brother Cody and his friends, Tony and Pete."

"You mean to tell me that I ran away from your brother and his friends?" Jessica said, with steam coming out of her ears.

The boys were laughing hysterically.

"We really got you." shouted Cody.

"Yeah right, I knew it was you the whole time," I said.

The boys made their way out of the woods, and in the light I could see what they were wearing.

My dad is a scientist at the university and he is always bringing home spare robot parts. The boys must have taken some of the parts out of Dad's home lab. They made some very scary masks out of the robot parts. They even glued fangs onto the mouths of the heads.

My brother was always pulling tricks on me. He and his friends thought they were so cool. Cody was only a year and half older than me, but he loved to boss me around.

"We really got you this time," said Tony.

"You didn't fool me," I said.

"Me either," said Jessica.

I could tell Jessica was scared out of her wits, but I'd had a feeling something was weird about those monsters from the start.

"We won't forget this." I said.

"Yeah, we are going to get you guys back, and it's going to be when you least expect it," said Jessica.

"Oh, we are shaking in our boots," said Cody, laughing.

"You can laugh all you want, Cody, but you're going to pay for what you did to us," I said.

It was getting late in the afternoon and Mom would be wondering where we were.

"Jessica, I'll see you tomorrow at school."

"Bye, Michaela, see you tomorrow."

I ran home as fast as I could, but Cody was already ahead of me, so I tried to run faster to catch up to him.

Chapter 2

My mom worked at a bank, but only while Cody and I were at school. She had always gotten us ready in the morning, and she was always at home waiting for us.

We lived only two blocks away from my school, and it took five minutes to walk home. As I ran around the corner, I could see Mom pacing in the front yard.

"Michaela, where have you been?" Mom asked.

"I just stopped by the woods with Jessica. We were looking for the nest of baby robins that I'd found the other day."

"Haven't I told you a million times not to go in the woods without your dad or me?"

"Mom, I was only in there for a few minutes."

"I don't care if it was for only one minute. There could have been some crazies in the woods looking to take kids away. You are grounded for a week. That means no TV, no e-mailing, and no phone calls for one week. And you have to come home directly from school every day. Now get inside, go to your room, and I don't want to see you until dinnertime. And make sure you finish all your homework as well."

My mother is so stupid. How does she expect me to learn anything if she doesn't let me go out and explore? If it was up to her, my life would consist of going to school, doing my homework, and chores, then going to sleep and doing it all over again. When does this leave time for fun? I bet she was born an adult.

"Michaela got caught, Michaela got caught, Michaela got caught," Cody was chanting outside my bedroom door.

"You'd better shut up Cody, or I'll tell Mom that you were there, too."

"Whatever. Mom doesn't care if I was there anyways."

"Oh, she'll care. And when Dad gets home I'll tell him that you raided his lab and took some of his robot parts."

"OK, OK, OK, I'll shut up," Cody said, as he ran into his room.

I finished my math homework and Mom yelled, "Kids, dinner is almost ready. Wash your hands and come downstairs."

I heard Dad pulling into the driveway. He always listened to me, unlike Mom, who always bossed me around.

"Daddy, you're home. There's a lot I want to tell you."

"Hi, Michaela, just hold on for one minute. I have to put my jacket away, and I really have to go to the bathroom. Traffic was a nightmare, and I drank three cups of coffee before I left school."

"All right, I'll wait until you're ready."

"Michaela, go and see what's keeping your brother," said Mom.

I stood at the base of the stairs, "Cody, get your butt downstairs. Right now."

"I could have done that. Go upstairs and get him."

I stormed up the stairs and whacked on his door, but I didn't get any response. So, I just walked in. Cody had his iPod on, and when he listened to music, he turned it up so loud that he wouldn't have heard cows running through the living room.

Cody saw me walk in and took off his headphones. "What do you want?"

"Mom said to come down for dinner."

"Yeah, yeah, yeah. I'll be down what I want to come down."

"Mom made her homemade pizza."

Cody's eyes lit up. He jumped off his bed, ran into the bathroom to wash his hands, then flew downstairs and asked Mom if she needed any help setting the table. Cody loved Mom's pizza, and he was willing to do anything to eat as soon as possible.

The smell of pizza enveloped the entire house. It smelled like the Italian bakery my parents used to take us to.

"Hi, Cody. Hi, Honey," Dad said as he made his way into the kitchen.

"Did you have a busy day at the lab?" Mom asked.

"Sure did. I've been working on this new robot that is taking up all my time. I can't wait to show you all it when I'm done."

Dad worked at the Boston Institute of Technology (B.I.T.). He was a scientist there and he had his very own lab. I loved it when Dad took me to work and showed me the projects that he was working on.

Mom took the pizzas out of the oven. Before I knew it Cody had already eaten four slices.

"You are a P-I-G, pig," I said.

Cody with his mouth full said, "Michaela, blob, bloob, blob up."

I couldn't understand him but I got the picture.

"OK, Michaela. What is this big news that you had to share with me?"

This was my chance. I was going to tell Dad everything that had happened in the woods. I imagined Cody being thrown into the corner of his room, grounded for life, and coming out of his room with gray hair and glasses. That would be cool.

"Uh, I got an A on my math test that we got back today."

I froze. It was my chance to tell him everything, but math came out of my mouth? Cody looked across the table and winked. I could always tell Dad some other time about the woods, when I really needed to get Cody. But come to think of it, I might have gotten in trouble as well, because I was not supposed to be in the woods, to begin with. I didn't care about Cody getting in trouble with Mom and Dad because I was already plotting my plan to get him back. I wanted Cody to forget about Jessica's and my plan to get him back.

"Michaela, do you have any plans on Saturday morning?" Dad asked.

"No, why?"

"How about just you and I go into Boston? We can go by the lab, and then I'll take you out to lunch."

"What are Cody and Mom going to do?"

"We have to go to the store to get Cody new pants. He has grown out of every pair, and Filenes is having a huge sale on Saturday," Mom said.

Cody hated getting poked and prodded by Mom at the store.

"I'm not going to the store on Saturday. I'm supposed to play baseball with my friends," said Cody.

"That's what you think," Mom said. "You are getting new pants and I don't want to hear one more word about it."

Cody ran out the room screaming and complaining.

"It's settled then. We all have our plans for Saturday," Dad said, with a big grin across his face. "I'm going to the living room. I need to lie down after eating all that pizza."

"Michaela, I want a word with you," said Mom after Dad had left. "What happened today can stay between you and me, but you must promise me that you will never go into the woods alone again."

"OK, I promise."

Maybe Mom wasn't so bad after all.

Chapter 3

Why do I have to sit in this stupid class and listen to this stupid teacher? I'm so bored. Who really cares who won the Battle of Little Big Horn? Do you think I'm going to have to know this when I'm older? No way.

Why couldn't Miss Webber have talked about something us kids wanted to hear about, like, where are you going this summer for vacation? Now that would have been cool. I'd tell her about playing video games, sleeping late, and swimming at the beach every day. But I still had to get through two more weeks of classes.

"What year did the Battle of Little Big Horn take place?" asked Miss Webber.

What? Was she talking to me?

"Michaela, I'm asking you a question," said Miss Webber, who had an extremely annoyed look on her face.

"They are horns that belong to a buffalo," I said.

All my classmates erupted in laughter.

I really knew what Miss Webber had asked me, but I loved to see my class bust up.

"Michaela, I'll give you one more chance to answer the question. What year did the Battle of Little Bighorn take place?"

"Oh, that's an easy one, it took place in 1876."

"Correct. Wouldn't it be a lot easier if you just answered me the first time?"

Yeah, it may have been easier for her, but what fun would it have been for me?

Jessica, who sat next to me then asked, "Hey Michaela, did you do the math homework for today?"

"Oh my God, I don't have it."

"If you want, you can copy mine at lunch time."

"That would be great," I said. "You always come through for me."

Jessica had always stuck up for me, even when kids were really mean to me. And they were mean to me a lot.

"OK, class, that's enough history for today," said Miss Webber. "It's time to work on cursive writing. Can you please take out your workbooks and turn to page 86?"

Finally, we got to work on something I actually liked doing. I had the best handwriting in the class. We worked on our handwriting for 35 minutes, and then the bell rang for lunchtime. I ran to my cubby, grabbed my lunch, and headed for the cafeteria. But I was stopped along the way.

"Did your mommy pack your lunch for you today?" asked Amy with a wicked grin on her face.

"What's it to you?" I asked.

"I just wanted to be ready to block my nose when you opened your bag up, and that horrible smell came out." Amy and her two friends started laughing.

"Yeah, whatever, Amy. Why don't you just run along with your two loser friends?"

I hated Amy. I hated her perfect smile and her perfect clothes. I didn't like her friends either, who did whatever she told them to do. Amy made fun of me every chance she got. What did I ever do to her? She was probably just jealous of me, because I made captain of the softball team that year, and she wanted to be the captain.

I made my way into the noisy cafeteria and spotted my table. Jessica went ahead, because her mom forgot to pack her lunch and Jessica wanted to get a salad before the line got too big. When I arrived, she already had her salad, and saved me a seat next to her, just like always.

"I just ran into Amy and her friends in the hallway."

"What did they want?" asked Jessica.

"They were giving me a hard time about my lunch again."

"Oh, they are just jealous. Their moms are so busy that they don't have time to make lunch for them. So they have to buy the gross school food every day and complain about it."

It was tuna surprise that day, and the lunchroom reeked of smelly fish. I was glad my mom had made my favorite lunch for me. My favorite sandwich in the world was peanut butter and banana with Fluff. Mom put some homemade chocolate chip cookies in for dessert as well, and an apple, which I had already eaten that morning.

"Jessica, can I get the math homework to copy?"

"Yeah, but what's your excuse for not doing it this time?" Jessica asked.

"I could lie to you and say my dog ate it, but you wouldn't believe that. So, I'll just tell you the truth. My cat ate it."

"Yeah, right."

"Well, you should believe it because that's what happened."

"OK, here it is."

Wow, for a smart girl she really was dumb. I couldn't tell her I just forgot to do the homework. If I had said that, then she wouldn't have let me copy the homework.

I copied the homework feverishly with my right hand, and stuffed my face with my left. Luckily the bell didn't ring until I'd finished the work.

Math class seemed to whiz by that afternoon, especially after I handed in my perfect homework assignment, and before I knew it, the end of school bell rang.

It was Friday, and I couldn't wait for the weekend, because Dad was taking me into Boston on Saturday.

Chapter 4

I couldn't wait to go to Boston. There were so many cool things to see at Dad's lab, and he said that he had a surprise to show me there. And he said I could pick out the restaurant that I wanted to go to for lunch.

"Michaela, are you ready to go?" Dad called.

"Yes. Yes. I'll be down in a minute."

I laced up my sneakers and ran down the stairs, only to trip over a baseball that was left on the stairs. *Bam*! I fell and hit the floor.

"Are you all right?" asked Dad.

"I think I'm fine but I broke my glasses."

"Again?" said Dad. "I'm going to have to shell out more money for new glasses. This is getting ridiculous."

I was always breaking my glasses, but luckily I had an old pair in my room.

"I'll just run back and grab my old pair."

"I'll be out in the car waiting. I'm going to have to talk to Cody about leaving his things lying around when we get back."

Oh good, maybe Cody would get in trouble. He deserved it after what he did to Jessica and me.

I grabbed my glasses, shut the door, and jumped in Dad's car.

"So, are you ready to see my new creation?"

"Yeah, I can't wait. Can you give me hint about it?"

"Maybe just a little one. You are going to get a very strange feeling when you see it."

"What kind of hint is that?"

"The only kind I'm going to give you."

The drive into Boston only took a half hour. I could surely wait that long. We went over the Bunker Hill Bridge and were almost there.

I fidgeted the entire ride. Dad finally pulled into the parking lot and we made our way into the university.

"Dr. Davis, I didn't expect to see you on a Saturday," said the security guard.

"I came in to show my daughter around. Michaela, do you remember Jim from your last visit?"

"Yes. Hi, Jim."

"Hi there, Michaela. Are you keeping your dad out of trouble?"

"I'm trying to."

"Great. Then you two go right in."

We thanked Jim and went down the corridor. The corridor smelled musty, and that smell reminded me of Nana's basement.

Dad's lab was located at the end of the long, dimly-lit corridor.

"Before we go in, you have to promise to close your eyes."

"I promise. Hurry up."

"OK, take my hand."

Dad unlocked the door and he led me in.

"You can open your eyes now."

"Holy crap." I couldn't believe my eyes. I was looking at my twin. It couldn't be. Could it? It was like looking in a mirror. The robot was the same height as me, had the same color hair, had glasses on and was wearing the kind of jeans that I wore.

"Michaela, you know you're not supposed to use that kind of language."

"Sorry, Dad, it just slipped out."

"Yes, I built my new robot to look exactly like you. I've been working on her for over two years. I really miss you when I'm cooped up at the lab, and I wanted to see you more. This is the next best thing."

"Can she talk?" I asked.

"I programmed her to sound exactly you. I recorded your voice and plugged your sound waves into the robot's voice box. Listen to this."

"Hi, my name is Michaela," said the robot. "What is yours?"

I couldn't believe it. The robot sounded exactly like me.

"Go on, answer her," said Dad.

"My name is Michaela, too."

"Nice to meet you, Michaela," said the robot.

"How come you built a Michaela robot and not a Cody robot?"

"Because I love you more than Cody."

"What?"

"I'm just kidding," said Dad. "I've actually just started working on the Cody robot. He should be done before you know it."

"How about Mom? Are you going to build a robot of her?"

"I'm afraid not. Mom said it would freak her out too much."

Come to think of it, it was a little freaky looking at myself but if it made Dad happy, then I was all for it.

"So, Michaela are you about ready for lunch, because I'm starving?"

"Yeah."

Dad told the robot to walk to the closet. She walked into the closet, and Dad pressed a few buttons under her shirt and she fell lifeless into the corner. It was weird, she even walked like me. I think she did, anyways. I've never seen myself walk.

We left the lab and made our way to the restaurant. I felt like an ant, ready to be stepped on. It was so crowded.

"Here we are Dad, Maria's Restaurant."

Maria's was my favorite restaurant in Boston. I ordered the chicken alfredo and Dad ordered the lasagna.

We anxiously waited for our meals but all I could think about was the robot.

"How did you get her to walk like me?"

"I took home videos that we had of you and programmed certain commands into the robot's main frame."

"I can't believe you got her so life-like."

"I had dreamed about making a robot life-like for years, and the technology finally caught up to my dreams."

Finally, after what seemed like ten hours, our meals arrived. We both ate every last bite of our meals and we were so stuffed that we wobbled out of the restaurant.

"Good pick," said Dad.

"It was awesome. I bet Mom and Cody are going to be jealous."

"Maybe they had a great lunch, too."

"It couldn't have been as good as ours."

We made our way back to the car and I was so tired from the meal that I fell asleep on the ride home. I woke up as we were pulling into the driveway.

"I can't believe that you made a Michaela robot," I said as I rubbed my eyes.

Chapter 5

"How was your weekend?" I asked Jessica.

"It was awesome. My dad took me into Boston, we went to his lab, and then we went to my favorite restaurant. It was so much fun."

"What's your dad working on at the lab?"

"You're never going to believe this. Dad is working on a robot, and the robot looks exactly like me."

"No way."

"Yes way, and the robot even sounds like me."

"That's so cool. I wish my dad had a cool job like yours. My dad is a boring lawyer who helps people get divorced."

Jessica's dad was actually really nice. He was Cody's baseball coach and Cody said he knew more about baseball than anyone that he'd ever met. I was never quite sure why she thought he was boring. I wouldn't mind being a lawyer when I grow up.

We made our way into school and before we arrived at class, I told Jessica about a plan I had to get the boys back.

"Now, you have to promise to keep this a secret. This plan has to be top secret in order to work."

"I promise. So what is it?"

"Well, my dad showed me this dyeing liquid he keeps in his home lab. The liquid is clear, but when it heats up, it turns bright purple."

"So what are we going to do with it?"

Jessica's eyes were lighting up. I could tell she was going to like this.

"Your father stores the team's equipment in your garage, doesn't he?"

"Yeah, so?" Jessica started to look suspicious.

"We're going to put the liquid into the sun block bottles, and when the boys start to get hot, the cream will turn bright purple."

"Awesome. They will freak out."

The bell rang and we grabbed our seats.

School was boring that day. Nothing great happened. Even Amy didn't bother me. That's because she wasn't there that day. She must have been home, sick.

I couldn't wait for the day to be over. Before I knew it, I got my wish and we filed out of school.

"I'll race you to my house," said Jessica.

We booked it to Jessica's house, and I beat her by half a step.

"You won again," said Jessica.

"Yeah, but just by a little. You'll probably get me the next time."

We went into Jessica's house and her mother was home.

"Mom, we are going to grab some stuff out of the garage and then play in the backyard," said Jessica.

"OK, I'll be shopping on the Internet if you need me."

We went into the garage and I pulled out the bottle of dye.

"Hurry up and get the tops off the sun block lotion," I told Jessica.

We opened up four bottles and poured the dye into them.

"Make sure you put the bottles back exactly how we found them," said Jessica.

We finished the job and went to the backyard to play catch with the softball. Jessica had a huge backyard. I think her dad made lots of money.

Mrs. Benson came outside and asked us to come in.

"Michaela, do you want to go to the baseball game with us? I was just talking to your mother on the phone, and she said that it would be all right. She said your dad and her would see you there."

"Yeah, thanks, that would be fun."

Mike came into the room, "Hey sis, what's up?" he asked. Jessica's brother, Mike, was on the team. He was good. He could hit the ball a mile, and he was the player who'd always hit home runs.

"Not much. Michaela and I are going to your game tonight."

"Oh, hi Michaela," said Mike.

Mike was cute. He was taller than my brother and he had blonde hair and blue eyes, just like Jessica. Mike was Cody's age and they both went to the middle school in town. I felt bad that Mike was going to use the sunscreen lotion, but it was the only way that we could get back at Cody and his friends.

"Your father is home," said Mrs. Benson. "Make sure you are all ready to leave for the game."

Mr. Benson asked for our help with the equipment. We grabbed the bags, loaded the van and headed out to the ball field. When we got there, Cody, Tony, and Pete were already at the field. My dad was sitting in the bleachers and I waved to him as we walked by.

"Good, all the boys are here," I said.

"I can't wait to see the look on their faces when the dye kicks in," Jessica whispered.

The boys grabbed the equipment and started warming up.

"Don't forget to put on the sun block lotion," said Mr. Benson. "The sun is still hot, and you don't want to get burned."

The boys slathered the lotion all over their faces and arms. The umpire yelled play ball and they took the field. By the second inning, the boys started to sweat.

"Wow, it's hot out here today," said Cody from his shortstop position.

"You're not kidding me," answered Mike from third base.

Then Tony yelled over to Cody, "Your face is turning purple."

"What are you talking about?" asked Cody. He then noticed his arm. "You're right, my arm is turning purple."

Cody started to freak out.

"Get this stuff off me," he said while scratching at his arms.

All the players were turning bright purple. And I mean a purple as deep as an orchard of grapes.

"Time out," yelled Mr. Benson. He then ran out onto the field.

"What is happening?" Mr. Benson asked, with an astonished look on his face. "All you guys are turning purple, do you feel all right?"

"I feel fine," said Pete. "But why are we turning purple?"

Jessica and I could not contain ourselves any longer. We burst out laughing.

"It was the girls," yelled Cody. "They must have had something to do with it."

Mr. Benson ran over to the bleachers. "Jessica, do you know anything about this?"

"I don't know what you are talking about," answered Jessica. But she could not stop laughing.

"This is your last chance. Tell me if you know anything about this."

"Yes, I do," said Jessica with a look of guilt on her face. "Michaela and I put dye into the sun block bottles."

"You did what?"

"We got the dye from Dr. Davis' lab and we put it into the bottles."

My dad stepped down from the back of the bleachers.

"Michaela, you stole the dye from the lab?"

"Yes, but it was Cody's fault. He scared me and Jessica at the woods, and we had to get him back."

"That is no excuse. You should never go into my lab. There could be harmful chemicals in there. Luckily the formula that you stole is not harmful. But there is one side effect."

"What is it?" asked Mr. Benson.

"The boys will be purple for one week. That's how long it takes for the dye to wear off."

"You are kidding me," yelled Cody. "We have to go to school looking like this?"

The game was called due to the purple scare. The umpire said it was the first time that he had called off a game because of players turning a color.

I was grounded for two weeks and so was Jessica. But it was worth it.

Chapter 6

The next morning I walked outside and there was a giant padlock attached to the front door of the garage. I guess Dad didn't want to me to go into his home lab anymore. One good thing about the padlock, it meant that Cody couldn't get into the lab anymore, and there would be no more monsters running around the woods.

I arrived at school. Everybody had heard about the baseball game. All the kids were laughing in the hallways, and kids that I had never met before were high-fiving me. It didn't bother me that I was grounded, because I was now having so much fun with my newfound popularity.

"Hey, Michaela, did the boys really turn purple?" asked one kid.

"Purple? They were purpler than the violet flowers outside of my house," I said.

I felt like queen of the school that day—at least until Amy came walking down the hallway.

"I hear you and your loser friend, Jessica, got into some trouble yesterday," Amy said. "I don't think it's funny what you guys did. I hope the players really get you two back."

"You're just mad because you're not smart enough to do something like that," I said.

"You call that smart? All you did was steal some dye from your dad. If it wasn't for your dad, then you'd never have done it."

"Yeah, at least I have a cool dad to steal something from."

I knew this would get Amy mad. She always complained about her dad.

"Michaela, I'm so sick of you. One of these days I'm going to get you. You're really going to be sorry then."

Amy stormed off down the hallway just as the bell rang for first period. We were in art class and the project was to make a series of paintings, staple them together, and hang them on the wall. I had completed my part of the painting and needed to staple mine to my classmate's, who was sitting in front of me.

"Hey, Seth, I'm ready for your painting," I said.

"Just one more minute," he said. "Then I'll be ready."

Seth was in most of my classes, and he was pretty cool. I had known him since kindergarten. I got my stapler ready.

"I'm done," Seth said. "Here you go."

"Thanks. How much do you trust me?"

"Why are you asking me that?"

"Would you put your finger in this stapler before I use it on the paintings?"

"Why would I let you do that?" asked Seth.

"Because I promise that I won't do anything to you? So, do you trust me?"

Seth looked confused at first, but he started smiling and said, "I don't know why I'm doing this but go ahead. I trust you."

I gently took his hand and placed his pinky finger in my stapler. I then pressed the stapler into his finger.

"What are you doing Michaela?" Seth screamed.

Blood started oozing out of his finger and onto the floor and he sprang out of his seat.

"What is all this commotion?" asked Miss Webber as she ran towards us.

Miss Webber grabbed Seth's hand and pulled the staple out of his finger. More blood dripped on the floor.

"Jessica, go get the school nurse," Miss Webber shouted.

Jessica ran out of the class and came back with the school nurse. The nurse had her first aid kit with her, cleaned up Seth's wound and placed a bandage on it.

"Seth will be fine," said the nurse. "It's only a small cut."

"Nurse White, can you inform the principal's office that they will be having a visitor," said Miss Webber.

Nurse White said that she would tell the office that I was coming and left the room.

"Michaela, you march yourself straight down to the principal's office," said Miss Webber.

I hoped that the principal was going to be easy on me. I sat waiting in his office for what seemed like ten years. Finally, the secretary told me to go in to see him.

"Michaela, do you realize that you could have really hurt that boy?" said Principal Morris. "What do you have to say for yourself?"

"I'm sorry. I feel really bad. I like Seth. I didn't mean to hurt him."

"I can't let this slide. I will be calling your parents and you have just earned yourself one entire week of after-school detention. And, I want you to apologize to Seth in front of the entire class."

"OK, I will."

The principal led me back to class and I apologized to Seth. Seth actually laughed about it and told me that he thought it was funny. He might have thought that it was funny, but what were my parents going to do to me?

Chapter 7

"Michaela, you just got in trouble yesterday, and now today I get a call from the principal," said Mom. "What are we going to do with you?"

Mom was angrier than I had ever seen her. I was really in for it this time.

"Go to your room and think about all the bad things you've been doing. When your Dad gets home we will talk to you."

I went to my room and plopped down on my bed. I was so angry that I wanted to get up and kick down my closet door. It wasn't my fault. I couldn't help myself and Seth had actually thought it was funny. I heard Dad's car pull up and I knew I was in for a big lecture.

"Richard, do you know what your daughter did at school today?" Mom asked as we all gathered in the living room.

"What did Michaela do this time?"

"She stapled a kid's finger. Luckily the kid is all right. Your daughter received afternoon detention for five days."

"Daddy, I didn't mean to do it. Seth thought it was funny."

"That's no excuse," said Dad. "You are now grounded for two more weeks. It looks like you won't be spending much time with your friends for a while. However, we will allow you to still play your softball games, because you can't let your team down."

I didn't argue with my parents, because I knew that I was wrong. Maybe I could let out some of my anger at gym class tomorrow. Every Thursday we played dodge ball. I loved that game.

I nearly missed school that Thursday because I overslept, after tossing and turning all night thinking about what I'd done to Seth. I just made it to school when the final bell rang.

"Are you psyched for gym class today?" asked Jessica.

"I can't wait. Today is dodge ball Thursday."

Gym class was the last period of the day and I could barely hold my excitement in during the first six periods. The bell rang for seventh period and I ran to the gymnasium.

"Today we will be playing dodge ball," said Mr. Jameson, the physical education teacher.

The class started chanting, *dodge ball Thursday, dodge ball Thursday, dodge ball Thursday.* Dodge ball was not just my favorite, but the entire class's as well.

"We need two people to be captains for the game," said Mr. Jameson. "Michaela and Amy will be the captains for today because they are the best leaders."

We chose the sides and I was able to get Jessica on my team. It seemed like I got the better of the two teams, but of course Amy thought otherwise.

"We are going to kick your butts," said Amy.

"You better shut up, Amy, because I'm not in the mood for you today," I said.

Mr. Jameson lined up the red rubber balls across the middle of the basketball courts.

"Each team line up against your wall and when I blow the whistle you may start playing."

I stared directly into Amy's eyes and began to get really angry. I couldn't wait to whip the ball at her. Mr. Jameson blew the whistle and we ran for the balls. Amy's team somehow got four out of five of the balls. I ran back and forth and ducked under one throw. The next throw I was able to catch and that knocked out one of Amy's players. Amy's team then knocked out two of my player's on their throws.

"I'm coming after you," I yelled to Amy.

I ran as fast as I could to the line and threw the ball as hard as I could towards Amy. But it sailed five feet over her head and it went off of the wall.

Amy quickly gathered the ball, "You will not escape my throw," she yelled.

Amy was able to corner me. She threw the ball and it sailed towards my head, but at the last second Jessica dove in front of it and saved me. She took the hit off of her stomach.

"You're awesome. Thanks, Jessica."

"Just get Amy," screamed Jessica as she stumbled off the court.

Both teams suffered more losses and the only two players left were Amy and me. The game was to be decided by one last ball. Mr. Jameson placed the ball in the middle of the court.

"Girls, when I blow my whistle, run for the ball. This will decide the winner of the match."

I had to get to that ball first. No way was I going to let Amy get to it. The whistle blew and I ran as fast as I could towards the ball. I dove at the ball and I was able to get to it just before Amy did.

"You are going to pay," I yelled at Amy.

I ran at Amy, wound up, and released the ball. The ball struck Amy's feet and it lifted her off of her feet. She hit the ground and I pumped my arm in the air.

"Michaela's team are the winners," declared Mr. Jameson.

My teammates ran onto the court and started chanting my name. I was so happy that I forgot about being grounded. Amy wasn't too happy. She bowed her head and went back to her teammates.

"We'll beat your butts next time," Amy yelled.

Who cared about the next game? We won, and that's all that mattered.

Chapter 8

I was running late for school again. No matter what I did, I could never get to school early. But that week I already had afternoon detention, so there was no way I could be late. Mom and Dad told me that I couldn't go into the woods without them, but the only way I could make it to school on time was to cut through the woods.

I ran into the woods. The morning sun was shining through the tree limbs and the ground was wet with morning dew. I had to be careful not to slip on it, but I was in a hurry. I hit a patch of wet leaves and landed in a bush. As I picked myself up, I found myself staring into the eyes of a hideous skunk.

I moved slowly because I didn't want to scare the skunk. At first he didn't seem to care that I was there, but then he made a loud hissing sound. The sound scared me. I forgot about being calm and raced away from the skunk. But I only managed to get about ten feet away when he let out a steam of spray. It was the worst smell in the world, like burnt stinky sweat socks and I thought that my nose was on fire. The stink went all over my body.

I raced out of the woods and stopped on the road. I couldn't stand to smell myself. My backpack, clothes and even my hair had the stink all over it. What could I do? I looked at my watch. I had only two minutes to get to school. I couldn't go back home now. Maybe no one would notice the smell. That was it. I would just pretend like nothing had happened.

I walked into school and immediately someone noticed.

"What is that awful smell?" asked Amy.

Suddenly all the kids were blocking their noses and running away from me. I ran into my classroom.

"What is that horrible smell?" asked Miss Webber. She walked over to me, "Did you get sprayed by a skunk?"

"Uh, uh, yes, I guess I did."

"You can't stay in here then," said Miss Webber. "Go down to the nurse's office and see what she can do."

I walked down to the office.

"Michaela, you can't stay in school today," said Nurse White. "I'll call your mother to come and pick you up. She's going to have to give you a tomato juice bath."

Oh great. I was going to get in trouble again.

Mom picked me up a little while later.

"Michaela, didn't I tell you that that you were not supposed to cut through the woods?"

"I know, but I was late for school. It's not my fault there was a stupid skunk there."

"That's no excuse," said Mom as she pulled into the supermarket's parking lot. "Wait here and I'll run in and get the tomato juice."

Mom came out with two bags full of juice and we raced home.

"Get yourself into the bath tub and I'll grab the can opener," said Mom.

Mom opened the cans and poured the juice into the tub. The juice felt squishy between my toes.

"Scrub it all over you," Mom commanded. "You're stinking the whole house up. I hope we can get the smell out of my car."

I massaged the juice into my hair. It was so gross. Oddly enough it made me hungry. I craved a big plate of spaghetti.

"This stuff is making me hungry. How long do I have to stay in it?"

"The nurse said that you have to stay in it for at least an hour to get rid of the smell."

The hour seemed like ten, but it gave me some time to do some thinking. I kept thinking about the robot. It was so cool that Dad had made a robot just like me. But how could I use this robot? It would be great to fool some people. Maybe they would think the robot was really me. I had to come up with a plan to use the robot to my advantage.

Mom came back and said, "Your hour is up. Let's see if the smell is gone."

Mom sprayed water all over me, rinsed the juice off, and then told me to scrub myself with soap. I rinsed the soap off and Mom sniffed me.

"I think the smell is all gone," Mom said. "You are lucky. Let's hope that getting sprayed by the skunk will prevent you from cutting through the woods."

I was already grounded for two weeks, so Mom said I already had enough time to think about what I had done. I think she felt bad for me.

The smell was finally gone. One good thing came from the incident though. I started to think about a plan to use the robot to my advantage. It wouldn't be long until I set that plan in motion.

Chapter 9

My week's worth of detention was finally over, and I had just finished one week's worth of my grounding. Hooray for Friday. I was sitting in my room that afternoon doing some homework, when someone knocked at my door.

"Michaela, I need to speak to you," said Mom. "You've been doing your homework every night just like you're supposed to. And we know that you've been cooped up all week, so tomorrow, when we go to the mall, we'll let you come with us."

"Thanks, Mom," I said, as I gave her a big hug.

That Saturday morning we all piled into the mini-van and made our way to the mall.

"You'd think it was Christmas," Dad grumbled as he drove up and down the lanes of the parking lot. "Cody, I see someone leaving that spot. I don't want any one else taking it, so jump out the van and stand in the spot until we get there."

Cody jumped out. He looked like a dork standing there waving at us, but Dad was happy because Cody saved the spot. We left the van, went into the mall, and joined the thousands of shoppers who were busy picking up their various items.

"Do we have to stay with you guys the whole time?" Cody asked Mom and Dad.

"If you and Michaela promise to stay together, we'll let you go off on your own for one hour," said Mom. "But you have to promise to meet us back at the food court."

"We promise," Cody said.

Staying with Cody was a pain, but it was better than staying with our parents the whole time. Cody didn't object to the idea especially after they said to meet back at the food court. It was getting close to lunchtime and he wanted to stuff his face.

"I want to go to Video Games Are Us first," said Cody.

"If we go to the video game store first, you have to promise to go to the Discovery store next."

We made our way to the video game store but I had to stop Cody.

"I can't go any farther. We have to stop at the restroom first."

"Oh, come on. Can't you just hold it until later?"

"I'm going to burst if I don't go. I'll yell and cry until we go."

"If it'll shut you up, then we'll go," Cody said as he pulled me along.

The hall to the restrooms was extremely long. We passed the groups of girls chatting on their cell phones and the toe-tapping men waiting for their wives. As we approached the doors to the restrooms, I noticed that the emergency door at the end of the hall was slightly open and smoke was coming into the hall.

"Check it out," I said to Cody. "The emergency door has a block at the bottom to keep it open. And why is there smoke coming in from outside?"

"Let's go see," said Cody.

I pushed open the door, but as we left the building I accidentally kicked the piece of wood outside. The door slammed behind us and a piercing alarm went off so we had to cover our ears. Just then I noticed a cigarette-smoking security guard standing there.

"What the heck are you kids doing?" asked the huge bald man. "I was out on my break smoking. Now you kids are really going to get me in trouble."

I then heard the siren of the fire trucks coming nearer and groups of people began filing out of the mall in a frenzy. They were screaming and yelling and looked confused.

"You kids need to come with me," said the security guard.

"Please let me go to the bathroom first. If I don't go, I'll burst."

"OK. Hurry up though, it's going to get crazy around here," said the security guard.

I went to the bathroom, ran out, and the security guard led us to the front of the mall.

Customers were huddling up in front of the mall entrances, and people were honking their car horns due to the backup in traffic that had begun. Just then the traffic parted and two shiny red fire trucks pulled up. The firefighters jumped off their trucks and ran towards the main entrance. The security guard, while dragging us, headed them off.

"There is no fire," said the security guard to the firefighters. "It was a false alarm. These kids tripped the alarm."

"It wasn't our fault," said Cody. "We noticed smoke coming into the corridor and we were worried that there might be a fire."

A tall red-bearded firefighter asked the security guard, "Is that a pack of cigarettes in your top pocket?"

"Yes, it is."

"Well, I bet you were outside smoking a cigarette, and that is the smoke the kids saw."

"Exactly," said Cody.

"I'm sorry," said the security guard. "I didn't mean to cause any trouble. I only went outside for two minutes. I didn't think anything bad would happen."

The firefighters made an announcement to the crowd.

"It was just a false alarm. Everybody can go back inside."

Many people were muttering under their breaths that this false alarm had interrupted their shopping. They seemed really unhappy. As the crowd thinned out, I noticed Mom and Dad running towards us, as the fire trucks sped out of the parking lot.

"We heard your story," said Mom. "It sounds like you guys were just trying to find out where the smoke was coming from."

"Look how much chaos you two have caused," added Dad.

"We are sorry," I said. "We didn't want the mall to burn down or anything."

"Even so, you have just earned one more week of grounding, and Cody you are now grounded for a week," said Mom.

"That's not fair," Cody screeched.

"We are not concerned with whether or not you think the punishment is fair," said Dad. "We're your parents and you'll obey us."

Mom and Dad grabbed us and took us back to the mini-van. As we were pulling away, I noticed the security guard talking to another man and he didn't look too happy. I bet you anything that the dumb security guard got fired.

Chapter 10

I loved teacher's curriculum day, because it meant I could get a whole day off from school. That spring it fell on a Wednesday, and Wednesday was the day Mom worked at the bank. My parents were OK with leaving Cody alone, but I knew after everything that I'd been doing, there was no way they were going to leave me with him.

"Michaela, get ready. Don't forget, you're going to work with Dad today," Mom said.

I didn't mind that plan. I loved going to Dad's lab.

I got ready as fast as I could, and Dad was waiting by the door ready to leave. I carried Dad's briefcase to the car and we left.

"Don't forget we have to pick up Jessica," I said.

We pulled up to Jessica's house. She was already waiting outside for us.

"Hi, Dr. Davis," said Jessica.

"Good morning," Dad said as we set off to the lab.

"Are there always this many cars on the road?" I asked.

"This is nothing," Dad said. "You should ride with me on a Friday afternoon."

We arrived at the lab after what seemed like hours.

"Hey, Jim," Dad said to the security guard.

"Michaela, you're back so soon with your Dad, and you brought along a friend this time," said Jim. "Don't you two have school today?"

"We lucked out. It's teacher's day and we get the whole day off."

"Well, have fun today," Jim said with an enormous grin on his face.

I couldn't wait to see the robot, and show it to Jessica. Dad went to the back of the lab and brought out the robot.

Jessica's face went bright red. "I can't believe it," she said. "It's your twin."

"Dad, turn her on so Jessica can hear her talk," I said.

Dad pushed the buttons under the robot's shirt and it came to life.

"Hello, my name is Michaela," said the robot.

"She sounds just like you," Jessica said.

"I'm very proud of this robot," Dad said. "It has taken me twenty years to perfect a life-like robot."

The door to the lab opened, and an ancient-looking man with a gray beard walked in.

"Dick, the staff meeting begins in ten minutes," said the man.

"Oh, I almost forgot about that," said Dad. "Dr. Williams, this is my daughter, Michaela, and her friend Jessica. Girls, this is my boss."

"Nice to meet you," said Dr. Williams. "Do you think you girls will be all right for one hour, while Dr. Davis attends the meeting?"

"Yes, we'll talk to the robot," I said.

"Ok girls, but do not leave this lab," Dad said as he walked out the door.

"Dad showed me how to program the robot," I said as I fiddled with its buttons.

The robot danced around the lab, and jumped up in the air.

"Wow, that's hilarious," Jessica said.

It hit me. I could send this robot to school to do my up coming history test. That would be awesome. I wouldn't have to study for the test, and I'd get an "A," for sure.

"Jessica, I just came up with an awesome plan."

"We need to send the robot to school in my place and she can take my history test for me."

"Oh, that would be so much fun," Jessica said. "But how are we going to get the robot from this lab to the school?"

"Dad always brings his projects home when he goes away. He is going away next week so we can test out our plan."

"We have a softball game on Sunday," Jessica said.

"Perfect. We'll send the robot in my place."

Dad came into the room after the hour was up.

"Did you have fun with the robot?" he asked.

"Yeah, I was even able to program her to do a dance for us."

"That's great," Dad said.

We watched Dad work for the next few hours, and before I knew it, it was time for us to go home.

"All right kids," said Dad. "That's enough work for the day. Let's get you kids home."

"Hey Dad, are you going to be bringing the robot home with you on Friday night?"

"Yes, I'm going away next week on business. Why do you ask?"

"Oh, no reason. I was just wondering."

Dad looked puzzled, but I don't think he suspected anything. It was only four days until Sunday and I couldn't wait to set my plan in motion.

Chapter 11

I woke up that Sunday morning after tossing and turning all night. Sunday was the day we were playing for the league championship in softball, and the day that the robot would win the game for my softball team. I was scheduled to pitch that day. This would be the perfect time to see if my friends could tell the difference between the robot and me.

I walked into the kitchen and saw Dad making coffee.

"I'll be riding my bike down to the game today. Is that OK?"

"Yes, your mom and I will be down later, closer to game time," said Dad.

"Is Cody coming to see me?" I asked.

"Yes, we already told him that he had to be home in time for your game," said Mom.

I was too nervous to eat breakfast so I skipped it. I went back to my room, grabbed my uniform, and ran out the back door. My plan was to get the robot to the game, with Jessica's help.

I ran to the garage, picked the lock, and went inside. The robot was in the corner behind the locker, just waiting to be turned on. I grabbed my uniform, and feverishly dressed the robot. I couldn't believe my eyes. The fit was perfect. Even my cap fit, without adjusting it. Dad really did make the robot to be just like me. Then I heard someone rustling outside the garage.

"Michaela, it's just me," said Jessica.

"You got me worried."

"Have you got the robot ready yet?"

"Yeah, I think so. Can you check her out, before I turn her on?"

Jessica inspected the robot.

"I can't believe your uniform fits her so well," she said.

"Dad made her exactly like me."

I pressed the three buttons and the robot came to life.

"Hello," it said.

"Hello," Jessica and I said.

"OK, don't forget the plan," I said to Jessica. "You and the robot will go to the game, on the bikes, and I will be hiding out in the woods watching."

"All right, I'll meet you there after the game."

Jessica and the robot got on the bikes and pedaled off to the game. I ran as fast as I could through my neighborhood, and hid in the woods. Through the trees, I could see Jessica and the robot warming up for the game. It looked like they were fooling everyone.

The parking lot filled up with cars and the ball field became packed with fans. The teams finished warming up and took to the field. We were the home team, so the robot started pitching first.

"Strike one," the umpire yelled.

The next pitch was thrown, and he yelled, "Strike two."

The third pitch was thrown and he yelled, "Strike three. You're out."

I couldn't believe it. The robot had struck out the first batter on three pitches. She then struck out the next two batters.

It was weird. I was looking at the robot pitch, and it was as if I was looking in the mirror. The robot jerked her pitching motion, just like I did. She even stuck her tongue out while pitching. I don't know how Dad got the tongue to look so real.

The ball field noise was so loud that it was probably heard all the way to Boston. Inning after inning, the robot kept striking out the side. The only problem was that my team wasn't scoring any runs, and the score was tied 0-0 after five-and-a half innings. We were looking good for the bottom of the sixth though, because we had the top part of our order coming to the plate.

Amy led off the inning with a single, our second batter struck out, and then our third batter popped out to the shortstop. The robot was the fourth batter. She walked up to the plate, hit dirt out of her cleats, then took a couple of practice swings and settled in at the plate. She stared straight at the pitcher's arm and waited for her delivery.

"Strike one," yelled the umpire.

The pitcher then threw the next pitch.

"Strike two," yelled the umpire.

The pitcher then threw the ball.

CRACK

The ball sailed over the left field fence. The robot rounded the bases, and my entire team was waiting for her at the plate when she crossed it. Everybody went wild. I couldn't believe it, my team were the champions. My teammates picked up the robot, put her on their shoulders, and ran around the field cheering.

Dad, Mom and Cody ran over to the robot too. They congratulated her, not even noticing that it wasn't me. I wasn't surprised that Mom and Cody were fooled, but I couldn't believe that Dad didn't realize that it was me.

The crowd started making their way to their cars. Jessica said goodbye to her parents, and the robot and Jessica waved to my parents.

Jessica and the robot then pedaled the bikes into the woods to meet me.

"Can you believe we won, and everybody thought the robot was you?"

"That's awesome, but we have to hurry to beat my parents home."

All the parents were talking after the game, so I knew that if we hurried it shouldn't have been a problem beating them home. Jessica and the robot jumped on one bike and I jumped on the other.

"Hurry up, Jessica," I shouted, as I pedaled as fast as I could.

We made it home in five minutes flat, then I grabbed the robot, and put her back in the exact same spot that I had found her in the garage. I stripped the uniform off the robot, and put it on, then ran out the garage, and locked the door. I then fell onto the driveway from exhaustion.

My parents and Cody pulled up into the driveway.

"Great game, girls," Dad shouted as he winked his left eye.

"Michaela, you have just earned some time off for good behavior," said Mom. "We are all going out to dinner to celebrate. Jessica, you are invited, too."

"Awesome," Jessica and I yelled in unison.

We sure fooled everybody. But I hoped the robot would pass her next big test, fooling everyone at school, including Miss Webber.

Chapter 12

"Can you believe we fooled all those idiots?" I said to Jessica that night in my bedroom after the softball game.

"It was a lot easier than I'd thought," Jessica said.

"What was the robot saying to our teammates?" I asked. I could only hear the umpire yelling and the crowds cheering.

"It was unbelievable," Jessica said. "The robot was saying things that you would say. I heard her saying, come on guys keep your head down, and that team will never beat us, because they play like five-year-olds."

"Wow, that's cool," I said. "You know what, we need to send the robot to school on Friday."

On Friday I had a big history test and did not want to take it. I hadn't memorized any of the facts that I had to. There was no way that I could pass that test.

"We already fooled everybody once. It shouldn't be hard doing it again, and the robot was so cool. It was nice to everyone." said Jessica.

"Even to Amy?" I asked.

"Yes, it treated everyone the same. Amy kept saying that she couldn't believe how nice you were to her."

"Wow, we really tricked them."

"So, what do you have planned for the robot on Friday?" Jessica asked.

"We're going to meet in the morning before class. I'll have clothes ready for it, and we'll all walk to school together."

Luckily, Dad was starting his new project and he would be leaving the robot at his home lab during the week.

"But this time I want to be inside the school, so I can see and hear everything the robot does."

"How are we going to pull that off?" Jessica asked with a puzzled look on her face.

"I have it all figured out. I have a note that I typed up on Mom's stationery, asking if my cousin can come to school with me on Friday."

"Your cousin is going to school with us on Friday?" Jessica asked.

"No, silly, I'm going to be my cousin." I said as I pulled out a wig from my closet.

"That's a great idea. Why don't you wear a dress, too? No one would ever believe that you would wear a dress to school."

That was true. The only time that I ever wore dresses was on holidays, and my mother had to pay me money to do it.

"Jessica, that's an excellent idea. I won't wear my glasses either."

"There is no way anyone will recognize you," Jessica said.

I pulled out the letter that I had typed up and asked, "How does the letter look?"

The letter said that my cousin from Chicago was visiting, and would it be all right if she spent the day at school with me.

"Jessica, you are good at signing people's names. If I show you my mom's signature, will you copy it on to the letter?"

"No problem. I'm the best at that kind of thing."

Jessica was a great artist. I knew it wouldn't be a problem copying my mom's signature.

"How do these look?" Jessica asked as she showed me three practice signatures.

"Perfect."

"Here I go, then." Jessica said as she signed the letter.

"That looks excellent. It looks exactly the way Mom would do it," I said as I looked over the letter. "Tomorrow I'll bring in the letter and we'll see if Miss Webber lets us bring my cousin to school. If she does, we are all set to go on Friday."

"You should find out something about Chicago, in case anyone asks you about home."

"That's a good idea. I didn't even think about that."

Jessica left and I surfed the Internet to find out about Chicago.

I arrived at school the following Monday to the loud cheering of my classmates.

"Michaela, you won the game for us," said Amy as I walked into my classroom.

All my classmates were shaking my hand.

"How come you were so nice to me at the game yesterday?" asked Amy.

"My mom told me I had to be nicer to my classmates, so I'm trying to make her happy," I said.

"Oh, you do everything that your mommy tells you."

"Shut up, Amy. You are a complete loser."

"I knew that you couldn't be nice for too long. You must have taken a nice pill yesterday."

I was going to snap back at Amy again, but I heard the classroom door open, and saw Miss Webber coming in.

"OK, class. Everyone settle down. I know you all had an exciting weekend, but we have a lot of work to do today."

Miss Webber could really be a drag. How were we supposed to settle down after winning the softball championship the day before? And how was I supposed to settle down after tricking all those people at the game?

"Our first lesson will begin in five minutes. Does anyone have anything they would like to discuss before we begin the day?"

"Miss Webber, I have a note from home that I need to give you," I said.

"Bring it up, please."

Miss Webber read the note and said, "So your cousin will be coming in from Chicago in a few days. We would love to meet her."

"Thank you, Miss Webber. My cousin is really looking forward to the trip."

"What's your cousin's name?"

"Kate. And she looks just like me."

"All right then. Please take your seat, Michaela."

I walked back to my seat and winked at Jessica. Only four more days until the real fun would begin.

Chapter 13

It felt like it took four years, not four days for Friday to arrive, but when that day finally arrived, I was ready to trick the entire school.

I went to the back of my closet, grabbed my red flowered dress, black sandals, and the blond wig that I had used the previous Halloween, and stuffed them into my backpack. I put on my usual jeans, t-shirt and sneakers outfit, then ran down the stairs. I got stopped in the kitchen.

"Hey, I'm psyched that it's Friday," said Cody.

"Me, too. I have a history test today, and I bet you anything that I'll get an A on it."

"You get an A? That's hilarious. You've never gotten an A on a history test."

"Well, I will this time. I bet you five bucks that I get an A."

"If you are so sure, how about betting ten dollars?"

"You've got a bet."

This was going to be the easiest money I ever made.

"I'm out of here," said Cody. "I'll see you after school to collect my ten dollars."

"I don't think so. I'll be the one with ten extra bucks to spend at the fair this weekend."

I sucked down a glass of orange juice as Mom walked into the kitchen.

"Wow, you're in hurry today."

"It's Friday, and the sooner I get to school, the sooner it'll be the weekend."

"You must be excited about the Spring Fair. Your dad has the biggest booth that he has ever had set up this year."

"I can't wait for the fair. It's supposed to be the best one yet."

Mom didn't suspect anything. She really thought I cared about the fair, but all I was thinking about was fooling everyone at school with my big switch.

"See you after school," said Mom as she grabbed her keys and left for work.

I waited until Mom pulled away and then went into the garage. It was odd because the door wasn't locked. I went into the garage, and I then noticed Jessica arriving.

"Are you ready?" asked Jessica.

"I think we are all set."

I dressed the robot, and then I put the girly clothes on.

"How do I look?" I asked Jessica.

"Good, but take off your glasses and put on the wig."

I took my glasses off, put them on the robot, and adjusted the wig on my head.

"Michaela, I can't believe it. You look a lot different."

"Cool," I said as I turned on the robot.

We arrived at school and passed our first test.

"Michaela, is this your cousin from Chicago?" asked Amy.

"Yes," answered the robot. "Her name is Kate."

"Hi, Kate. I hope you're a lot nicer than your stupid cousin, Michaela," said Amy as she went to her seat.

"OK, class, take your seats," Miss Webber said as she entered the classroom. "It looks like we have a guest today. Michaela, can you introduce your cousin to the class?"

"This is my cousin, Kate, from Chicago. She is staying with us for the weekend."

"Hello, Kate," said Miss Webber. "Can you tell us something about yourself and your city?"

"I'm in the fourth grade, I have a little brother, and the Cubs are my favorite baseball team. It's a lot colder in Chicago than it is here, and we have the best pizza."

"Welcome to Boston, Kate. You'll have to try our pizza. It's a lot different than Chicago style. It's thin and crispy. Now class, we have a history test to take. I hope you are all prepared."

My class let out a loud groan as the test was passed from front to back. The exam took thirty minutes, but the robot was finished in ten minutes.

"Time is up," said Miss Webber. "Pass your exams forward. I will correct them at recess."

As we passed them forward the recess bell rang.

Everybody was so worried at recess about how they did, but I wasn't worried at all. I knew the robot had aced it.

The bell rang and we filed back into class. Then Miss Webber handed back our exams, and I looked over the robot's shoulder after it received the exam.

"Oh my, Michaela, you got an A. You got every one of the questions right," I said to the robot.

I was so happy, but I had to keep my happiness in. I didn't want anyone to suspect anything. The rest of the morning flew by and before I knew it, we were in the cafeteria waiting in line for our lunch.

"I'll have the hot dog," said the robot to the hair-netted lunch lady.

The robot grabbed the plate and stuffed all the food down her throat.

"Another please," the robot said as she stuffed the next plate of food down her throat.

The entire line of kids waiting stopped talking, and was staring at the robot in disbelief.

"Another please," said the robot again.

The robot did not stop eating. She ate eight hot dogs before me and Jessica pulled her out of the line.

"What has gotten into you?" I asked the robot.

I didn't want the robot to blow my cover. We grabbed our lunch and sat down at the table.

"This pizza is no good at all," I said.

Amy overheard me.

"Oh, so Chicago pizza is so much better than Boston's. I knew it. You are just like your cousin. Nothing is good enough for a Davis."

"Amy, shut your mouth or I'm going to kick your butt." I could not stop myself from getting angry.

"You are going to pay for that," Amy said as she jumped on my back and wrestled me to the ground.

Straight away, the robot pulled Amy off me. The robot threw her across the table and picked me up. Amy came back for us, but the robot blew at her, stopped her in her tracks, and pushed her back. Amy then ran out of the cafeteria in tears.

"Michaela, you saved your cousin," said one of my classmates.

"It was nothing," said the robot.

"It was something," said Jessica. "Amy would've beaten your cousin up."

All the kids were cheering when the teacher on lunch duty, ran over to us.

"OK kids, the fun is over," said the teacher as he tried to stop all the commotion. "Get back to your tables and finish your lunch. And a few of you can expect a call down to the principal's office, after I speak with him."

We were halfway through Miss Webber's lecture on continents when the announcement came on the speaker.

"Michaela Davis, Kate Davis, and Amy Chadwick report to the principal's office."

We got up from our desks and made our way to the office.

"I shouldn't get in trouble. It was your stupid cousin's fault," said Amy.

"You're crazy. You started the whole thing," said the robot.

We got to the office and sat down in front of the secretary. We didn't wait for very long when we all got called in.

"Mr. Casey told me everything that happened in the lunch room. Amy and Michaela, you have both earned afternoon detention for three days, starting Monday afternoon."

"It wasn't my fault," said Amy.

"I don't care who started the fight. You two are always at each other, and you're both responsible for what happened. And, Kate, I understand that you're in town visiting and you'll be going home soon."

"Yes, sir," I said.

"Well, I hold Michaela responsible for your part in this. I just hope that you don't act this way at your school."

"No, sir, I never get in fights."

"Well, off you go. And, I better not see you three in my office again."

I wasn't too happy because, I was going to have to serve the detentions. There was no way that I was going to risk sending the robot to detention those three days.

We went back to class, but the day was almost over. The bell rang fifteen minutes later, and we ran out of school.

"Are you going to the fair tomorrow?" one of my classmates asked Jessica.

"Yeah, I'll be going with the Davises. I'll see you there."

Chapter 14

It was a perfect day for a fair. There wasn't a cloud in the sky, and it was so warm that I was able to wear shorts for the first time that year. We were all looking forward to stopping by Dad's tent because he said that he had something special in store for everyone.

"Can you believe all the rides they've got?" asked Jessica.

"I think there's even more than last year. They added the *Whip*. It spins you around wicked fast, and you feel like you're gonna fall out and hit the ground."

"I'm not going on that ride," said Jessica.

"Don't be a chicken. I went on it at the beach, and it wasn't that bad."

I was actually scared to go on the ride too, but I figured if I could get Jessica to go on it then it wouldn't be too bad.

Then I noticed Amy.

"Michaela, where's that dumb cousin of yours today?" asked Amy. "I have some unfinished business with her."

It was bad enough that I had to see Amy at school and softball, but I had to see her at the fair, too. Why couldn't our town be a bigger place?

"She went into Boston with my aunt and uncle to see the Red Sox."

"She's lucky, because I would've kicked her butt if I'd seen her today."

"How about taking me on then?"

As we were about to start fighting, Mr. Benson showed up.

"Girls, is everything all right here?"

"Yes, Mr. Benson," we answered.

"We wouldn't want our star softball players not getting along, now would we?"

"I was just leaving," said Amy.

As Amy walked away Jessica said, "Let's try every game that we can."

"OK, let's start with skee ball."

We were rolling those balls for so long, our arms were starting to kill us, but we wanted to win the biggest prize that we could.

I turned around and noticed Mike walking toward us.

"Michaela, how did you get way over here so fast?" asked Mike. "I just saw you on the Ferris wheel, and there's no way that you could've beaten me over to here."

"I don't know what the heck you're talking about. I've been over here for like an hour."

"You're crazy," said Mike. "You were on that Ferris wheel less than five minutes ago."

"If you don't believe me, then ask your sister," I said.

"Jessica, how long have you guys been over here?"

"A half hour, at least," Jessica answered.

"You two are both crazy," said Mike as he stormed off.

We had the skee ball fever and we kept playing and playing and playing. I heard Cody's voice coming towards us.

"How did you get over here so fast?" asked Cody

Oh no, another stupid boy asking us dumb questions.

"We just saw you riding on the bumper cars. There's no way that you got over here so quickly."

"Cody, you are looney tunes. Look at all these tickets coming out of the machine. I had to have been here for a long time, because there are at least two hundred tickets there."

"You must have a twin then, because I know I saw you," said Cody as his friends joined him as he laughed.

Something fishy was definitely going on. But what could it be? We stopped playing skee ball and cashed in our tickets.

We had to get to the bottom of this mystery. Someone was playing a trick on us. But who could it be?

Mom spotted us through the crowd at the prize table.

"Girls, I've been looking all over for you. Dad has a special presentation in ten minutes at his tent and he wants us all to be there."

We arrived at the tent as crowds of people were making their way into it.

"Wow, there are tons of people coming to see your dad's presentation," said Jessica.

"Yeah, check out the sign," I said.

UNVEILED TODAY, A MODERN MARVEL OF SCIENCE,
SURE TO THRILL ALL

"Let's get inside so we can see what he's going to unveil," Jessica said.

We made our way into the tent and took our seats next to Cody and his friends, who were in the front row, saving seats for me, Mom and Jessica.

"This is so exciting," Mom said. "I don't even know what your dad is going to unveil."

I had a feeling it was going to be the robot, but I didn't let anyone know what I was thinking.

Dad and his assistant rolled out a huge crate and dropped it in the middle of the tent and said, "Ladies and gentlemen, I have the future inside this box."

The crowd cheered and I could feel excitement in the air.

As Dad pried open the box, I heard gasps in the crowd.

"It's Michaela," shouted Mike.

"No, it's her twin," shouted Amy.

"Let me explain folks," said Dad. "I've created an exact replica of my daughter, Michaela. Watch as I turn the robot on."

Dad pressed some buttons behind her shirt and the robot said, "Hi, my name is Michaela, it's nice to meet you all."

The robot jumped in the air, spun around, walked up to the seats, and shook hands with the crowd.

"So, who was playing skee ball?" Cody asked Dad. "Was it the robot or the real Michaela?"

"You'll have to ask your sister," said Dad.

"I was playing skee ball," said the robot.

"No, you weren't," I said. "It was me. Can't you people tell the difference between that pile of bolts and me?"

I was headed for trouble. I just knew it.

Then I spotted Miss Webber in the crowd.

"Michaela, I would like to have word with you outside the tent. If that's all right with you, Mrs. Davis."

"Be my guest," said Mom. "Maybe you can talk some sense into my daughter."

Miss Webber led me outside the tent. "I'm only going to ask you once, and I want you to tell me the truth. Was it you who took the history test? Or was it the robot?"

I really wanted to lie, but I figured it was no use.

"I'm sorry. I wanted to get an A so badly that I sent the robot in my place."

"You are unbelievable. I should fail you in history and not allow you to go up to the fifth grade next year."

"Please, Miss Webber, I'm sorry. I promise I can make it up to you. I can't be kept back."

"The only way that I could allow you to move onto the fifth grade is if you take the history test over and receive at least a B."

"How the heck am I supposed to do that? If I could've gotten a B, I would have taken the stupid test myself."

"That is your only option. You have to take the test on Friday of this week."

I was doomed for another year of fourth grade. I just knew it.

Chapter 15

I studied all week for the history test, and because I had three after school detentions, I was able to study the entire time I was there. I also studied every night after dinner until I went to bed.

The test was scheduled for after school on Friday, and when Friday arrived, it seemed to drag by so slowly. All I could think about was the test. There was no way that I wasn't going to get a B. I was doomed.

It was the last day of school and all my classmates were excited, but I couldn't join in. The end of the day finally came, the bell rang, and everybody else ran out of class.

"Can you believe it? Summer has finally come," said Jessica. "Good luck on the test. I just know you'll pass it, and be joining me in the fifth grade next year."

"I hope so," I said nervously.

Miss Webber walked up to my desk and asked, "Are you ready for the exam?"

"Yes, I'm ready."

I started the test. It wasn't as hard as I had thought it was going to be. Maybe that week of studying had actually paid off. I kept checking the clock for time, and finished the test with five minutes left to go.

"Miss Webber, I'm finished."

"OK, pass your exam to me and I'll look it over."

"Are you going to correct it now?" I asked.

"Yes, but you'll have to wait out in the corridor until I'm finished. I'll call you in when I'm done."

I walked out into the hall. To my surprise, Dad was standing there.

"Hi, Michaela."

"What are you doing here?"

"I wanted to see how you made out on the test."

"Thank you. I'm so nervous." I was sweating bullets, but I felt a little better now that Dad had arrived.

We waited for ten hours. OK, maybe it was only ten minutes, but it felt like ten hours.

Miss Webber opened the door. "Come on in, I'm ready for you. Oh, hello Dr. Davis, I didn't expect to see you today."

"I wanted to see how my daughter made out," said Dad.

I sat down behind the desk and Miss Webber passed the test to me, while Dad stood next to me with a nervous look on his face.

"Oh my God, I got an A. I'm so psyched."

"Congratulations, honey," said Dad. "I knew you could do it."

"Good job," said Miss Webber. "You'll be able to go on to the fifth grade now."

I screamed as I jumped from my desk.

"Can you please sit back down?" asked Dad.

I was so excited that I almost couldn't sit down, but I took my seat and said, "I'm happy. Can't you tell?"

"We knew that you were a much better student than the grades that you have been getting," said Miss Webber. "Your dad came to me with a plan to try and help you realize that you could get better grades if you just applied yourself."

"Michaela, do you think that I didn't know that you stole the robot out of my home lab? I have hidden cameras all around the garage."

"You're kidding me. I didn't know that," I said.

"I don't want anyone stealing my life's work. After your first break-in and the robot's performance, I figured you wouldn't stop using it. So when Miss Webber called your mom and me about your, so-called cousin's classroom visit, we knew then that you were up to no good. So I devised a plan with Mom and Miss Webber."

"So Mom knows everything, too?"

"Yup, we were all in on the set up. It was easy. I was the one who left the garage door open for you that day."

"I did find it strange that the door wasn't locked."

"We really needed Miss Webber's help," said Dad as he turned towards Miss Webber. "Thank you for everything."

"No problem," said Miss Webber. "I had a lot of fun doing it. You know, I used to be an actress in college, and I miss that sort of thing."

53

"It's not nice to fool people," I said to Dad.

"We were at the end of our rope with you. It was either this, or ship you off to boarding school."

"In that case, thank you for pulling the trick on me," I said.

I said bye to Miss Webber, and walked out the school.

"Just so you know, I put the robot into storage," Dad said. "She did her job, and now it's time to get my next project going."

"I'm going to miss that robot. Hey, how about when I get to college you can make another robot for me, so I can have her take my math tests then?"

Dad didn't even answer me. He just rolled his eyes, and shook his head.

"Come on," I yelled to Dad as I ran from the school. "Can you catch me?"

Dad tried to catch me, but I was too far ahead. I felt so much better knowing that I could actually get an A, if I tried as hard as I could.

I ran across the playground and chanted.

"School's out for summer…"